The Farmer, The Devil and The Turnip

Original title:
The Farmer, The Devil and The Turnip

Copyright © 2023 Creative Arts Management OÜ
All rights reserved.

Editor: Kristo Villem
ISBN 978-9916-676-89-9

The Farmer, The Devil and The Turnip

By Clement Portlander

"The Farmer, the Devil, and the Turnip" is a classic Estonian fairy tale that has been passed down through the generations. It tells the story of a poor farmer who is struggling to provide for his family in a small village. Desperate for a better life, the farmer is approached by the Devil, who offers to help him become wealthy in exchange for the farmer's soul.

The Devil gives the farmer a magic turnip seed and tells him that it will grow into a giant, golden-colored turnip that will bring him great wealth. The farmer is skeptical, but he plants the seed anyway. To his surprise, the turnip grows into an enormous vegetable that is larger than any he has ever seen.

Excited at the prospect of selling the turnip at the market and becoming wealthy, the farmer sets out to find a buyer. However, when he arrives at the market, he finds that no one is willing to pay a fair price for the enormous turnip. Disappointed and frustrated, the farmer returns home empty-handed.

The Devil, who has been watching the farmer's efforts from afar, decides to take matters into his own hands. He approaches the farmer and offers to buy the turnip for a large sum of money. Thinking he has finally found a buyer, the farmer eagerly accepts the offer and hands over the turnip.

But the Devil has no intention of paying for the turnip. Instead, he laughs at the farmer and tells him that he has tricked him into selling his soul for nothing. The farmer is horrified and begs the Devil to take back the deal, but the Devil refuses.

Feeling defeated and helpless, the farmer goes to bed that night and cries himself to sleep. The next morning, he wakes up with a plan. He goes to the Devil and tells him that he has changed his mind and wants to keep the turnip. The Devil, thinking he has won the deal, agrees to let the farmer keep the turnip and leaves.

The farmer, relieved to have outsmarted the Devil, returns home and celebrates his victory with his family. From then on, the farmer is able to sell the turnip for a high price at the market and becomes one of the wealthiest men in the village.

As for the Devil, he is left empty-handed and bitter at the farmer's clever trick. He vows to never again underestimate the intelligence of a simple farmer. And so, the story of the farmer, the Devil, and the turnip becomes a cautionary tale for all those who might consider making a deal with the Devil.

The moral of this story is that we should be careful of the choices we make and the deals we agree to. It is easy to get caught up in the promise of wealth and success, but we must be mindful of the potential consequences. In this case, the farmer was able to outwit the Devil and come out on top, but not everyone is so lucky. It is important to think carefully about the long-term consequences of our actions and to be aware of those who may try to take advantage of us.

The moral of this story is that we should be careful of the choices we make and the deals we agree to. It is easy to get caught up in the promise of wealth and success, but we must be mindful of the potential consequences. In this case, the farmer was able to outwit the Devil and come out on top, but not everyone is so lucky. It is important to think carefully about the long-term consequences of our actions and to be aware of those who may try to take advantage of us.

The story of the farmer, the Devil, and the turnip serves as a reminder that we should never underestimate our own strength and intelligence. It is a tale that has been passed down through the generations in Estonia, reminding people of all ages to be cautious and to always be on guard against those who may try to deceive us.

Overall, "The Farmer, the Devil, and the Turnip" is a classic fairy tale that teaches valuable lessons about the importance of being careful and thoughtful in our actions. It is a story that will continue to be passed down through the ages, serving as a reminder of the lessons it teaches.

It is a reminder to always be cautious and to never underestimate our own strength and intelligence, no matter how difficult our circumstances may seem. It is a tale that encourages us to think carefully about the choices we make and to be aware of those who may try to take advantage of us.

In a world where it is easy to get caught up in the pursuit of wealth and success, "The Farmer, the Devil, and the Turnip" serves as a reminder to stay grounded and to never lose sight of our values. It is a story that will continue to inspire and educate people for generations to come, reminding us all of the power of determination and resourcefulness in the face of adversity.

CPSIA information can be obtained
at www.ICGtesting.com
Printed in the USA
LVHW052009020223
738427LV00014B/1069